CARVED FROM SAND

A SAILING ROMANCE STORY

M. L. BUCHMAN

Buchman mixes adrenalin-spiking battles and brusque military jargon with a sensitive approach.

— PUBLISHERS WEEKLY

13 times "Top Pick of the Month"

— NIGHT OWL REVIEWS

Tom Clancy fans open to a strong female lead will clamor for more.

— *DRONE*, PUBLISHERS WEEKLY

Superb! Miranda is utterly compelling!

— *BOOKLIST,* STARRED REVIEW

Miranda Chase continues to astound and charm.

— BARB M.

Escape Rating: A. Five Stars! OMG just start with *Drone* and be prepared for a fantastic binge-read!

— READING REALITY

The best military thriller I've read in a very long time. Love the female characters.

PRAISE FOR M. L. BUCHMAN

A fabulous soaring thriller.

> — *TAKE OVER AT MIDNIGHT,* MIDWEST
> BOOK REVIEW

Meticulously researched, hard-hitting, and suspenseful.

> — *PURE HEAT,* PUBLISHERS WEEKLY,
> STARRED REVIEW

Expert technical details abound, as do realistic military missions with superb imagery that will have readers feeling as if they are right there in the midst and on the edges of their seats.

> — *LIGHT UP THE NIGHT,* RT REVIEWS, 4
> 1/2 STARS

Buchman has catapulted his way to the top tier of my favorite authors.

> — FRESH FICTION

Nonstop action that will keep readers on the edge of their seats.

— *TAKE OVER AT MIDNIGHT,* LIBRARY JOURNAL

M L. Buchman's ability to keep the reader right in the middle of the action is amazing.

— LONG AND SHORT REVIEWS

The only thing you'll ask yourself is, "When does the next one come out?"

— *WAIT UNTIL MIDNIGHT,* RT REVIEWS, 4 STARS

The first...of (a) stellar, long-running (military) romantic suspense series.

— *THE NIGHT IS MINE,* BOOKLIST, "THE 20 BEST ROMANTIC SUSPENSE NOVELS: MODERN MASTERPIECES"

I knew the books would be good, but I didn't realize how good.

— NIGHT STALKERS SERIES, KIRKUS REVIEWS

SIGN UP FOR M. L. BUCHMAN'S NEWSLETTER TODAY

and receive:
Release News
Free Short Stories
a Free Book

Get your free book today. Do it now.
free-book.mlbuchman.com

Other works by M. L. Buchman: *(* - also in audio)*

Action-Adventure Thrillers

<u>Dead Chef</u>
One Chef!
Two Chef!

<u>Miranda Chase</u>
Drone*
Thunderbolt*
Condor*
Ghostrider*
Raider*
Chinook*
Havoc*
White Top*
Start the Chase*
Lightning*

Science Fiction / Fantasy

<u>Deities Anonymous</u>
Cookbook from Hell: Reheated
Saviors 101

<u>Single Titles</u>
Monk's Maze
the Me and Elsie Chronicles

Contemporary Romance

<u>Eagle Cove</u>
Return to Eagle Cove
Recipe for Eagle Cove
Longing for Eagle Cove
Keepsake for Eagle Cove

<u>Love Abroad</u>
Heart of the Cotswolds: England
Path of Love: Cinque Terre, Italy

<u>Where Dreams</u>
Where Dreams are Born
Where Dreams Reside
Where Dreams Are of Christmas*
Where Dreams Unfold
Where Dreams Are Written
Where Dreams Continue

Non-Fiction

<u>Strategies for Success</u>
Managing Your Inner Artist/Writer
Estate Planning for Authors*
Character Voice
Narrate and Record Your Own
Audiobook*

Short Story Series by M. L. Buchman:

Action-Adventure Thrillers

<u>Dead Chef</u>

<u>Miranda Chase Origin Stories</u>

Romantic Suspense

<u>Antarctic Ice Fliers</u>

<u>US Coast Guard</u>

Contemporary Romance

<u>Eagle Cove</u>

Other

<u>Deities Anonymous (fantasy)</u>

<u>Single Titles</u>

The Emily Beale Universe
(military romantic suspense)

The Night Stalkers
MAIN FLIGHT
The Night Is Mine
I Own the Dawn
Wait Until Dark
Take Over at Midnight
Light Up the Night
Bring On the Dusk
By Break of Day
Target of the Heart
Target Lock on Love
Target of Mine
Target of One's Own
NIGHT STALKERS HOLIDAYS
*Daniel's Christmas**
*Frank's Independence Day**
*Peter's Christmas**
Christmas at Steel Beach
*Zachary's Christmas**
*Roy's Independence Day**
*Damien's Christmas**
Christmas at Peleliu Cove

Henderson's Ranch
*Nathan's Big Sky**
*Big Sky, Loyal Heart**
*Big Sky Dog Whisperer**
*Tales of Henderson's Ranch**

Shadow Force: Psi
*At the Slightest Sound**
*At the Quietest Word**
*At the Merest Glance**
*At the Clearest Sensation**

White House Protection Force
*Off the Leash**
*On Your Mark**
*In the Weeds**

Firehawks
Pure Heat
Full Blaze
*Hot Point**
*Flash of Fire**
Wild Fire
SMOKEJUMPERS
*Wildfire at Dawn**
*Wildfire at Larch Creek**
*Wildfire on the Skagit**

Delta Force
*Target Engaged**
*Heart Strike**
*Wild Justice**
*Midnight Trust**

Emily Beale Universe Short Story Series

The Night Stalkers
The Night Stalkers Stories
The Night Stalkers CSAR
The Night Stalkers Wedding Stories
The Future Night Stalkers

Delta Force
Th Delta Force Shooters
The Delta Force Warriors

Firehawks
The Firehawks Lookouts
The Firehawks Hotshots
The Firebirds

White House Protection Force
Stories

Future Night Stalkers
Stories (Science Fiction)

ABOUT THIS BOOK

LOCAL GLOUCESTER ARTIST MORGAN HENRY BUILT A career carving sand. Upon the arrival of a magnificent racing yacht off the beach, he alters his latest contest entry to match. Little does he know that his past skippers the boat.

Mary Elizabeth sailed away from Gloucester and made her name on the ocean racing circuit. She never once looked back. Yet for reasons beyond her understanding, she returns.

On the beach, in a sand sculpture conceived by a boy but carved by a man, she discovers that her past and her future are more connected than she could possibly imagine.

1

MORGAN FLICKED THE KILL SWITCH AND THE POUNDING stopped. His arms were buzzing from manhandling the gas-powered jumping jack tamper for much of the morning. Thank God he was done with that phase of the build. The early phases of building a competition-level sand castle required much more than a plastic shovel—a stage he'd never truly enjoyed. He had his sand prepped. Now the fun began.

Shoving back the earmuffs, he was assaulted by the clatter and engine roar of others near him. Three of the other fifteen competitors were still compacting their sand. The rest were shoveling more sand into their next layer of frames prior to more compaction.

Only Romero had already shed the topmost layer of forms and begun shaping. Nobody sculpted sand as fast as Romero. It was a pity he didn't like Romero's work. He had a whole Mexican Day of the Dead macabre vibe. He also colored his sand with clays and food coloring, which was technically acceptable, but felt wrong to Morgan.

He was a traditionalist down to the soles of his callused feet and believed that the coloring hid the actual artistry of the carving itself.

Fifteen feet up in the air atop his sculpture offered an exceptional view. This was his home sand, Good Harbor Beach, Gloucester, Mass. He'd grown up less than two miles away and had spent much of his youth riding his bike here. Half a mile of smooth beach sand, hard-packed by the tides, backed by dunes and with the whole sweep of the Atlantic straight ahead. Interrupted only by tiny Salt Island to the north, which connected to the shore by a rocky sandbar at dead low tides.

They had four days to build their sculptures, and it was already the morning of the second day. But the weather was perfect, a light overcast and only a vague breeze. The sand wouldn't dry too fast.

He knelt down and poked his fingers into the topmost compacted layer. Almost no give at all—just perfect.

The organizers had done a good job, trucking in rougher glacial sand for better holding ability. Beach sand was typically too smooth, all of its sharp, holding edges worn off by the pounding of the sea. Exceptional sand, one percent water, and hard compaction. He liked the feeling of this one.

He glanced down the line. Sure enough, the pinnacle of Romero's sculpture was taking on the shape of a battered top hat. So predictable. Morgan's theory was to stay fresh by constantly changing and growing his artistic style.

The long beach was busy for a weekday. Of course, it always was in the summer. He spotted a cluster of bicycles up by the wooden walking bridge from Eastern Point that arced over the salt marsh drainage channel. How many times as a kid had he parked his own bike there?

Mom had always told him to get a life. Dad had been a professional surfer in his youth and understood Morgan's need to be at the beach. But with them gone, Morgan knew he was straining the limits of what his career could be. It had taken a decade to build up to going pro. Sponsors now paid his way to competitions all over the East Coast—the visiting master sculptor. More money on the side for teaching classes. He'd even done a couple of West Coast competitions on his own dime but almost always ended up in the money. First prize could net him ten grand for a week's work. Too bad there weren't competitions like this one every week. Of course that way lay travel burnout and severe sand rash.

He was at some tipping point. Balanced as lightly as one dry sand grain atop another. Morgan had no idea what lay to either side. After this week, nothing remained to tie him to Gloucester except memories.

Focus on the here and now.

This beach was a good one without being a zoo like Coney Island or Hampton Beach up in New Hampshire. The latter was thoroughly epitomized by a hundred kitsch shops packed tighter than wet sand, including seventeen t-shirt shops in the main mile (he'd lost count after that and hadn't bothered to check out the back streets), at least as many overpriced restaurants, and even a deep-fried Oreo stand of all madness. Not his kind of scene.

Here at Good Harbor there was the hot dog and ice cream concessions stand, and nothing else. Rolling grass dunes, tidal marsh, and an incredible stretch of beauty. It was a foolish investment for the parks department, any income draw from the spectacle of the competition should be shared over a range of merchants. But this beach was well isolated from the rest of the retail in the area. Not his bother.

As he looked out to sea, a big sloop eased up toward the beach. Its lone mast seemed to etch the sky. The dark red hull and long lines made it look incredibly fast even as it came up into the wind and dropped an anchor. The rattle of the chain dropping overboard reached the beach during a chance pause of the various power tampers around him. He noticed that his wasn't the only pair of eyes that appreciated the boat. Growing up around Gloucester Harbor, he knew a purebred ocean racer when he saw one.

He looked down at the sand below his feet.

Morgan had initially planned to do Venus on the half-shell. Part Botticelli's *The Birth of Venus* and part the Philip José Farmer spoof novel of Kurt Vonnegut's character Kilgore Trout.

Now?

Again he eyed the lovely boat offshore.

There wasn't time to break down the forms and restack the sand.

But...

If he heeled the boat over to shift the mast to the side, he could carve that beauty out of what he already had.

Almost.

One more bucket. He'd need one perfect bucket of sand atop his current structure for the masthead. He glanced over at Romero working feverishly on his hat brim. One bucket would also make his own sculpture taller than Romero's by several inches, making it the tallest on the beach. Yes, he was good with that.

There was a lot of excess sand in the lower layers that he'd built with a different design in mind, but he'd think about that when he'd carved down far enough.

One more good look at the boat, just in case it left before he was done. Once it was firmly fixed in his mind, he clambered down the tiers hauling the jumping jack tamper with him. Mixing the perfect bucket of sand was second nature. Hauling the sixty-five-pound bucket fifteen feet in the air was as well.

A glance at the boat, he doublechecked the bucket's position for the new design in his mind's eye, and flipped it into place. As he worked to ease it free, he saw in his memory that a single figure had been diving off the side of the big ocean racer.

2

_____

MARY CAME ASHORE ON THE WARM HAVEN OF SAND AND wanted to simply lie there hugging it.

At the end of her trans-Atlantic race, she'd never actually gone ashore in New York. She'd meant to. After placing second in the solo race from Calais, France to the Brooklyn Bridge, she'd definitely planned to. There would have been good parties after the crossing. And she hadn't placed second in any *mere* women's division; she'd placed second overall to Thierry Montagne who was a masterful skipper. Masterful enough to beat her by thirty-seven minutes after the long crossing.

He had stepped over onto her boat on arrival, offered her a hug, and held her hand up to the cheering crowd that had packed the Brooklyn waterfront park. It had been kind, and he was always kind, except between the starting gun and the finish line when he was a ferocious and highly skilled competitor.

But then potential sponsors had come aboard. And newscasters. And boat geeks who began poking through everything that was hers. And women telling her that she was the perfect symbol of the modern powerful woman. And—

She'd shooed them all away, let slip the lines, and sailed toward home before the third-place finisher had passed the Verrazzano-Narrows Bridge. It was stupid, she knew. The sponsors alone were a key means to continuing to do the one thing she understood and loved.

But she wasn't anybody's symbol of anything. She was...herself.

Once here, not possessing enough patience to unship the dinghy, she had dived over the side and swum ashore.

In the shallow water, she now sat as she often had as a child, chest deep in the water, the low waves only occasionally splashing against her chin. There was something different about the water here. It simply felt right.

Straight ahead lay nothing until the Azores and the bulge of Africa. At her back lay her home town. She hadn't been back to Gloucester in a long time.

Mary tried to imagine why she was back at all. Her parents were gone. Her friends were other sailors, not the now total strangers from Gloucester. Even Vincenzo her first sailing instructor had died of old age, slipping beneath the waves of sleep and never reemerging, to give him his sailorly metaphor. His daughter had sent Mary the scrap album he'd kept of all of her races. *All* of them, even ones she hadn't recalled right back to her days ruling the Mass Bay Sailing Junior Championships.

She'd visited him only the month before he'd died, but hadn't been back in the decade since.

So why now?

For an overpriced hot dog and a pre-packaged ice cream cone?

Could be.

She climbed to her feet and did her best to squeeze the water out of her hair. Really facing the land for the first time, it was as if nothing had changed. The wide beach, low salt-grass dunes behind. She knew that beyond that was the most expensive parking lot for a long way around. But the city pumped some of that money back into the beach; the sand was perfectly groomed except for a thin line of seaweed at the high tide line.

And inland...

She cocked her head and heard her neck joints crack.

Great wooden structures were lined up along the beach. Some over a story high, all roughly pyramidal in form. She saw someone had carved what looked like a black, actually black, battered top hat; his body blocking what he was working on below that.

Some were still shoveling sand, a few were breaking open the upper layers of their structures. She hit the concession stand, where the hot dogs looked so All-American that she ordered two, which would give her indigestion later but she didn't care. With one slathered in mustard and relish, and the other in ketchup— because only the grossly crass mixed all three—she went back to sit on the dune edge and watch the sand sculptors.

These were serious folks. Nobody was scooping together a bucket of wet sand and scraping a hole in it, about her level of sandcastle mastery.

Up close, she could see that Mr. Top Hat was shaping a grinning gray-white skull. At least she hoped it would be grinning when he reached that far.

A woman down the row cursed when she accidentally batted her prepared sand tower with the framing board she'd just removed, and created a small cascade of sand off the exposed face. After careful inspection of a drawing, she wiped her brow and proceeded to remove the other three sides. *Damage fixable.*

Near to where she'd landed, a long, rangy man with dirty blond hair to his shoulders trapped by a red bandana worked on the tallest of the piles. He had a beard just thick enough to not be a scruffy Captain Jack Sparrow pirate. Standing high in the air, he kept looking out to sea.

Looking toward her boat, the *Niles P.* She'd named it for the pond on the East Gloucester peninsula where she'd swum so often as a kid.

He wore no shirt, showing off his good muscles. Then he reached into his toolbelt—Captain Jack with a toolbelt was a nice combo—pulled out a palette knife and began carving. With quick confidant strokes he began cutting away at the cylinder of sand that topped his structure. It didn't take a genius to see her mast top emerging from the sand.

Except with far more detail than would be visible from this far away. The head block pulleys appeared rapidly from the sand. With a different tool, a wooden school ruler wielded like a saw, he made tiny marks along the exposed edges that would be the wire stays. That was a crazy level of detail, especially considering the huge amounts of sand trapped inside the lower plywood tiers.

He was almost frantic as he broke off the first layer of forms and tossed them down, nearly landing them on her toes.

"Sorry," he mumbled, but kept working without really turning.

It seemed that he was shedding an immense amount of sand. Mr. Top Hot and Creepy Skull was carving away small layers, but Captain Jack was shedding whole slabs, like the calving glaciers she'd seen in Greenland. Mr. THCS had been well ahead of the Captain when she'd arrived. But every time he paused to check his art against his drawing with level and tape measure, the man copying her sailboat in sand never hesitated. He was soon farther along despite all of the extra carving.

Perhaps he'd changed his mind when he saw her boat. Her boat certainly hadn't been there when he'd been piling the sand up.

Partway down the sail, just even with the spreaders, he froze. "Dammit! What was the number?" He glared offshore at her boat as if he could read the number on the furled sail.

"Thirty-four," she called up to him.

"Thirty-four what?" he turned around looking for the voice that had spoken to him, except he was scanning the sky around him at his level, not looking down at the people below. She was not the only one come to watch the carving, even at this early stage.

"Thirty-four is the number on my sail."

"Your sail?" He finally looked down at her. "Madonna

Mother of God." His jaw went slack. And that's how she knew the boy now grown into the pirate.

"You haven't called me that since grade school, Mr. Morgan Henry the Backward Pirate." Which had been her nickname for him. He'd taken great pride in almost being Sir Henry Morgan, the real pirate's namesake. It fit; he'd grown up to look rather piratical. Calling him the backward pirate had helped keep him in his place as a boy. Not really—unlike her, he'd been irrepressible—but she'd liked to think of it that way back then.

"Mary Elizabeth Thomas," he breathed it like a prayer. He'd always liked that her first and middle name had matched Sir Henry Morgan's wife.

It had led to a great excuse to tease each other mercilessly as they were growing up. Of course, Sir Henry had married his first cousin, also a Morgan, but what did they know about genetics back then.

"Wait!" He swung an arm to point out to sea and almost knocked the top off the sail he'd been carving. "Your boat?"

She nodded, and bit into her hot dog. Mary wasn't quite sure where the first one had gone, but this second one tasted damn good. Summers spent here as a little girl flooded back. She'd never belonged, but being with others even though she rarely spoke had been better than the achingly empty Niles Beach backed by the eight or ten mansions that owned its length.

He looked like a string puppet. First staring down at her, then twisting to look out at her boat, then back to her, and finally down at the vast pile of sand he stood on.

The backward pirate wasn't the gawky kid she

remembered. He'd been bullied plenty in school for his light build and sharp mind. She'd been a jock, already winning sailboat races by the time she was eight. A misfit, but winning for the school had been her protective shield. He'd had nothing except his artistic flair, which had always attracted the worst attention. Their mutual teasing was the closest either of them probably had to a friendship growing up.

Until her parents had shipped her off to Milton Academy starting in seventh grade. They hadn't wanted a kid underfoot and Milton had the best sailing program of any prep school up to her parents' hoity-toity standards. Losing her one semi-ally, her only protection at Milton had been to be the best. She'd never been a straight-A student, but nobody beat her on the water—ever.

She hadn't thought of the backward pirate much since, having done her best to block Gloucester out of her mind.

This time when he stared at her once more, she saw no sign of the gawky kid. He was studying her, not as a surprising piece of his past fetched up like a battered bit of driftwood but as if he was trying to memorize her.

"Could you drop your right shoulder a bit?"

She raised it as if she was the *Hunchback of Notre Dame* and he laughed.

"You always were a contrarian. Just drop it, please."

"Well, because you said please," she dropped it all the way until she was slouching against the sand like a melted Dali clock.

He laughed then called down, "Hold that for a sec."

Mary was tempted to move simply to annoy him, but

he was no longer looking at her. Instead he was intently studying the sand below his feet.

At a loud curse from two sculptures down, Mary jolted upright.

Morgan didn't react at all except to mutter softly, "Saw that coming."

The woman who had smacked the top layer of her sand tower with the board was staring at the cascading collapse of the exposed layer as whole sections of sand sloughed off and spilled over the lower tiers to land on the beach below.

3

———

Morgan's attempts to reconcile the grown-up Mary Elizabeth, the sailboat, and the yet unworked sand tower beneath his feet wasn't happening.

He couldn't begin to count the times he'd thought of her. She'd been his one friend, a fact he hadn't known until she was gone. His only touchstone of sanity beyond the front door of his family home. He in a crappy house out with the other broke artists of Rocky Neck had always had support and laughter, if not much money. She in her majestic Niles Pond Victorian where nothing was happy. What a difference a mile made.

She hadn't even come back for the double funeral of her parents. Some company had cleared out the house with no sign of her. One day up for sale and gone the next.

Her hair was still sunlight blonde and her eyes crystalline blue but Mary had grown into her angular face. The girl, always so serious and intent, now had elegant features. As the wet t-shirt and sleek one-piece underneath showed, she still retained the power that had always radiated from her once she'd discovered sailing and become a workout queen.

That the gorgeous racing boat anchored offshore, with no sign of anyone else aboard, was hers somehow made sense. Racing across oceans fit Mary Elizabeth right down to the, uh, ocean's floor. Maybe. Not really.

No, the only thing that truly made sense in his head at the moment was the sand. He'd always understood the sand.

And now, with perhaps more clarity than he'd ever had in his life, he could see exactly what waited to be exposed in the layers below.

"Please don't go anywhere," he whispered, then selected a small, triangular cake icing palette knife to etch the number thirty-four into the sail before moving to break away the next lower set of frames. Again he almost dropped them on her where she sat below.

4

———

At some point, she handed him a chocolate ice cream cone.

"Nutty Buddy. I always loved these." He peeled back the paper and bit into the hard chocolate-and-nut topping.

"I remember."

That brought him the rest of the way back from wherever he'd gone. The really good sandcastles sucked him in, until he lost all track of time and place. Until there was only himself and sand.

Taking a spray bottle in his free hand, he circled the sculpture looking for dry spots. He'd broken his way down through four tiers of plywood forms—eight vertical feet done, past halfway. He had the jib and main sail formed as if they were drawing full wind. A spritz here, a spritz there. That should be enough to keep it stable through the night.

The night?

He twisted to look to the west. The sun was gone

beyond the dunes and the hill past that. The thin overcast had stuck, and the far horizon glowed in an arc of red.

"Wow!" he rolled his shoulders, which ached but in a job-well-done sort of way, then clambered down the last two layers to look up at what he'd achieved so far. The sails were close to the theoretical limit for sand. He'd made the base of each thick, he'd had to, but from either side he'd held the illusion of the curve drawing to the wind.

Spreaders could only be a suggestion, several feet of sand sticking straight to the side simply wasn't possible without illegal artificial supports.

Tomorrow. Tomorrow, he'd start to carve the body of the boat and...

"I'm heading home."

It took him a moment to shake loose the image of the grand Victorian on Niles Pond. "Oh, to your boat."

"Yes. Maybe I'll see you tomorrow."

"I'll be right here."

She nodded, and with a wave was striding off into the low surf to swim back out to her boat.

Yeah, he licked where the Nutty Buddy was melting over the backs of his fingers making them all sticky.

Yeah. Reconciling the return of Mary Elizabeth Thomas was something that was going to take a lot more work than any sand sculpture.

5

SHE SHOULD SIMPLY SAIL AWAY. IF SHE HAD HALF A BRAIN, she would. Why the hell had she come back here anyway? To stir up all of those oh-so-happy memories she'd spent a lifetime blocking out?

Pacing the length of her boat, she began her routine nightly check when not under way. The main and jib were properly stowed. The bungee cord was on the genny halyard so that it wouldn't slap against the aluminum mast in the night. Her three-sixty-degree at-anchor light was shining bright white. She set the depth gauge to wake her if the anchor slipped and she drifted into shallow waters. Weather radar, forecasts, and barometer all predicted a quiet few days.

Everything was shipshape.

Except her.

Sixty feet she paced up one side of the deck and down the other but couldn't come to rest. When she finally forced herself to lie down in the cockpit, she watched the sky, a star here, another there through gaps in the overcast. Though she knew the night sky well, there was rarely a large enough clear area at once for her to identify them. Yet she watched for hours until the cool evening finally drove her below deck to her bunk.

The seagulls, who were stupid enough to think she might have been a fishing boat and greeted her arrival so loudly, had long since flown off to sleep elsewhere.

She'd been done with Gloucester long before her parents had shipped her to Milton. A mere hour from home, and not once had they come to see her race. They were too lost in their own misery. By the time of her graduation, she doubted they were capable of making the journey at all. She'd only gone home once, that first Christmas. It was not a mistake she'd ever repeated.

Alcohol Poisoning, and Gunshot Wound read the official death certificates when they'd reached her during her first stint as navigator in the Sydney Hobart Race. Mom drank herself to death and Dad must have realized that he couldn't survive with no one left to fight with. He'd been sober enough to shoot himself, but not sober enough to do it well. It must have been an ugly way to die, slow and alone with Mom's corpse beside him.

The family money had been deep enough, the property valuable enough, the estate antique enough, that even this boat had not made a significant dent in her net worth. She could sail a long time yet before she'd have to think about money, if ever. She was the most winning woman on the world racing circuit. Sponsors, even the ones she'd jilted at the New York dock, would gladly line up at her least show of interest.

So, why had she sailed here to Gloucester of all places?

The night offered no clues. She fell asleep near midnight, marked by the half moon clearing the horizon to spread a ghostly glow across the thin cloud cover.

6

MORGAN WATCHED FOR HER ALL DAY. MARY ELIZABETH hadn't come to the beach. He'd know her walk in a heartbeat among the hundreds who strolled along the sand. Watching her walk away from him to dive into the sunset sea last night had anchored that firmly.

She walked as she had as a child, with a determination and an assuredness of direction as clear as a laser beam. The body had changed, very nicely, and the long flow of blonde hair trailed off her shoulders as it always had. But her walk had been stamped as clear as a thumbprint upon his artist's memory.

While she might be hidden, the boat remained—anchored close off the beach. Once or twice he though he spotted movement aboard but it was always gone before he could be sure.

Instead he focused on the sand. Romero caught up with him as he carved his way down and Morgan had to keep stopping to be sure of the image in his head. No, actually while he kept stopping to see if Mary had come ashore and to make sure she hadn't left.

Patricia had rebuilt the top tier of her sculpture and was only now beginning to carve. At first he'd thought she was also carving a sailboat, but soon the fin became clear. It was going to be an orca—he should have known. She loved her cetaceans. He wondered what it would be eating this time, as they almost always were. Seals, dolphins, even the occasional octopus. A tad grisly, but it gave it an immediacy that he knew the crowds always appreciated no matter how much they cringed at the realism of her fabulous technique.

For others, the high turrets of several fairy tale castles were coming into being. Those competitors were lucky Marcus wasn't here; his castles combined medieval battlements, luscious fantasy, and occasional Escheresque modern whimsy that occupied the mind long after the sand had fallen. He was the best casteller living as far as Morgan was concerned. He was also in Italy this week.

Maybe if he too had done castles, or any one thing consistently, he'd have a career like Marcus'. But he hadn't. Every sculpture was a unique creation ripped from who-knew-where. He knew where this one came from though.

In the other direction down the row, for he was near the middle, a leaping fish attempted to look airborne but instead looked quite scared. A Greek Parthenon two past that. A stepped Inca pyramid in which the roughness of stone and the details of climbing ivy were taking the simple structure to the next level. Perhaps too simple to win, but elegant nonetheless.

A newcomer was fated to doom as he worked to erect an Egyptian obelisk made of sand. There simply wasn't enough width below to support the height and angle he was carving. Not even a mix with a few parts of food-grade glue would hold it up. Morgan gave it a practiced assessment. It might make it until end of day, but the humidity was supposed to fall tonight and the obelisk would dry and be gone by morning. Too bad, it was pretty work right down to the chiseled look of the hieroglyphs.

On his own sculpture, he had two tiers to go, the last four feet of the fifteen. The sails towered a full story above him, looking truly as if they were racing across the sea.

He wished Mary was here to ask for her permission, but was also glad that she wasn't so that he didn't risk receiving a no.

Morgan built up a small section near the stern of the boat and began carving her hair caught in the wind.

7

────────

MARY SLIPPED ASHORE BEFORE THE DAWN TO SEE THE sculptures. She kept the wide-brimmed sunhat pulled low, she'd certainly missed it yesterday sitting so long in the sun and watching Morgan.

Today she'd be gone before they unlocked the gates and anyone arrived on the beach. Only a napping guard remained to ward off any vandals. The scattering of inevitable morning joggers on the hard sand marred the morning stillness. She'd be over the horizon before full sunrise, leaving this world behind for good.

The call yesterday had decided her. She'd up-anchor and head for Miami. It was time for a change and the timing couldn't have been better.

Most of the US Olympic team had already been training for months at the US Sailing Center on Biscayne Bay, but that didn't worry her. She was still carving her future, not protecting her past achievements. She'd slide in and simply outsail anyone who came after her.

They wanted her badly enough that she'd been able

to dictate the terms; they'd try each other on for thirty days and see what they thought. No harm no foul if she chose to sail away—though she assumed that she'd never be invited back if she did. If they decided she wasn't the winner they needed? Well, she wasn't worried about that.

It was time, *past* time for a change of pace. For two years she and the *Niles P.* had taken on the solo racing circuit all over the world. She hadn't done a full circumnavigation yet, and still didn't know if she really wanted to or if it was merely a new hurdle to check off some imaginary list. Time to join other sailors, hone her technique. Refresh her thinking.

But when she should have upped anchor and turned south, Mary hadn't. She'd been riveted all through yesterday, able to see the sails of her boat forming beneath Morgan's fast-moving hands. They rose from the fine white sand like the lovely racing boat the *Niles P.* was.

Morgan hadn't been visible for most of yesterday afternoon. He'd made quick work of carving the lower hull and echoing the clean lines of her boat. The rest of the day he'd spent working on the shore side of the sculpture. She knew this was the final day and that the judging was this evening, but she planned to be well out to sea and cruising south by then. She wasn't above having a private look; it was her boat after all.

Maybe she would carve him a note in a pile of discarded sand to wish him well. That too could wash away with the first rain. Then her past would be fully dissolved.

She slid her dinghy up on the dark sand, threw out a small four-pound Danforth lunch hook, and kicked its flukes into the sand to keep the anchor in place. Besides, she should really hike up to Jeff's Variety Deli or the grocery store and load up on some fresh supplies for the long sail south. It would be against the prevailing wind and current, summer was not the time to be sailing south opposite the flow of the Gulf Stream. But neither had it been the time of year to race a North Atlantic crossing— and she'd managed that nicely enough.

She put Miami at four days in ideal conditions, which this wasn't, and had told them to expect her in ten for tryouts. She'd make it in six. Maybe seven.

Mary appreciated the smooth lines of her sailboat rising from the sand as she approached Morgan's sculpture from the seaward side. He had carved neat waves all along the base to mask the inward curve of the hull where he'd needed a broader base for more support.

It was when she came around the other side that she went stock still.

Difficult to see in the low sunrise light driving in from the east, the landward side of the sculpture was in deepest shadow.

As her eyes adjusted, she made out the boat's skipper. Morgan hadn't used either the hunchback figure she'd mocked him with nor the recumbent mermaid she'd offered afterward.

Instead he'd taken the classic Gloucester fisherman, shrouded in his Sou'wester and clutching the ship's wheel and replaced it with *her*. Her hair coiled in tangled confusion at the strong wind of his imagination, some strands plastered across her cheeks. She faced the sea with...something.

Desperation or dismay would be most likely, but Morgan had made a different choice. He'd given her a half smile. Not as if she was ready to battle the sea, or was ever dumb enough to think such a thing was possible. A sailor *survived* the sea, never beat it. It was...

She wasn't sure.

Glancing at the time, she shrugged on her knapsack, followed the passage through the dunes, crossed the parking lot, the road beyond, and climbed the hill to the grocery store.

The beach parking lot attendant was already unlocking by the time she returned, but if she hurried, she'd be gone before the first cars had parked and unloaded.

Across the lot, through the low dunes on the rough boardwalk, and...Morgan was already there. His bicycle was tossed atop the pile of discarded plywood forms and his concentration was wholly on the sculpture.

He had a barber's lather brush in one hand, a tiny scraping tool little bigger than a scalpel in the other, and, in one corner of his mouth, a clear length of surgical tubing.

As she watched, he brushed at a strand of her rendered-in-sand hair, then blew a small blast of air through the surgical tube to remove the least bit of loosened sand. She didn't know how, but she could see the difference in the areas he'd gone over already. They were sharper in some way she couldn't discern. In a way that...brought her to life.

"What are you doing to me?" She hadn't meant to blurt it out that way.

Morgan took a careful step back from his sculpture before turning to look at her, the clear plastic tube clamped in his teeth like a writer might chew on a pen while thinking. "Good morning, Ms. Mary Elizabeth."

"Good morning, Captain Backward Pirate. What are you doing to me?" She waved a hand unsure if she was indicating his incredible attention to detail, the look on her statue's face that she still couldn't equate with her own, or something inside that she refused to think about.

"I'm shaping you in sand. I hope that's okay. You weren't around to ask, and you do have the most beautiful face, Mary."

"I can see that. That you're using my face. The latter part of that statement only makes me question your sanity. No. I meant—" But what did she mean? He saw her in a way that she'd never seen herself.

Again she studied the expression on her doppelgänger's features and didn't know what to make of it.

"You were always my ideal of beauty. I'd have known you anywhere."

She couldn't have picked Morgan out of a crowd. The small boy with the smart mouth that was always getting him in trouble was in no way reflected in this man before her. She knew the boy. The man? Not even a little. Yet the more she looked at her figure in sand, the more she thought that perhaps he knew more about her than she did herself.

"I'm sorry, it's really too late to change. I can try, but I don't think it will work. I should have—"

"It's okay, Master Pirate. It's okay," she cut off his rush

of words. "It's just...weird seeing myself there in sand. Looking all..." She shrugged. "Maybe I spend too much time alone at sea. Using words? It's not something I do very often."

"You really race solo in that beast?"

"Mostly. Yes. The last two years exclusively. I'm going to be changing that soon."

He nodded sagely, as if he had a deeper wisdom, and turned back to continue his work. It was complete—to her unpracticed eye—with an entire day ahead of him. Yet every place he touched her likeness was better as he moved past it.

"Need a hand?" He asked without turning.

"A hand? I can carry my own groceries." Though she'd gone a little overboard and the pack was heavy. Vegetables, bread, cookies, as well as the more normal pasta and canned goods. There would also be a Jeff's Variety and Deli Italian Cold Cuts sub if she hadn't wolfed it down for breakfast on the walk back to the boat. She should have ordered two. That was a local taste she'd miss.

8

Mary Elizabeth Thomas was always a logical girl, Morgan mused, no surprise that she was still that way as a woman. He decided that the collar line of her Sou'wester should fall a little lower down her neck, she had a great neck. He selected a round-cornered rhombus Venetian plasterer's trowel from his tool bag, and reshaped the entire curve of the jacket. With an offset cupcake icer, he extended the hint of a curve made by her jugular vein, then blew air to clear the flaked-away sand.

A careful spritz of water, from a full foot back so the merest mist wetted the surface, and he studied the result. Yes, it was her.

"You've changed, and haven't," he didn't turn to look at her. It wasn't that he didn't need to—he didn't as she was so firmly fixed in his mind. It was that he didn't quite dare.

"Oh this should be good." And that hint of the old teasing tone they used to share was back.

He moved on to the shape of the Sou'wester where it

would be plastered against her shoulder. "You still interpret everything in the most immediate way. *I have groceries, they're heavy, that must be what he's talking about.*"

"You don't know me." But after a long moment he heard the knapsack hit the sand with a clank of cans.

"No, but I knew you. Closest thing I had to a friend, I studied you a lot. I don't think we can change that much." With her shoulder properly in place, he stepped back to study the angle of her arm as she gripped the wheel. He'd pedaled out to the tall bronze statue of the Gloucester fisherman along the Boulevard before sunrise this morning to make sure it was clearly fixed in his head. Did Mary see how much of that determination was in her as well?

"You remained the artistic boy following his own vision no matter what it drew down upon your head?"

He paused without turning.

"Sorry," she said quietly. "That came out sounding wrong. It was a skill I always admired in you. Your willingness to be yourself and to hell with all consequences."

And wasn't he paying the price now? The American medical system had caught them, stepping in to help only after Dad's cancer had wiped out all of Mom's and his own savings. Mom had died within weeks of Dad, the life had simply gone out of her. The house was gone to pay off the last of the debts. He now had a bicycle, his tools, and a spot on a buddy's couch.

He should have...he didn't know what. Saved more? Become a world-class cancer doctor to have found a miracle cure for Dad? Become a grief counselor who could have saved Mom?

Instead he carved sand.

A strange, ephemeral existence so easily erased by wind, rain, or simply time.

Morgan shook himself and did his best to return to the carving. If he won this one, he could afford to pay a little rent for his couch space, eke it out to the next job or competition. And then?

"The consequences can really suck."

9

MARY STUDIED MORGAN'S BACK AS HE WORKED. HIS shoulders had slumped as he'd paused, slumped like Atlas' from holding up the world.

Then, somehow, when it looked as if it might crush him, he shrugged it off and returned to sculpting her. She watched for hours as he worked over every shape, going grain-by-grain—except her face. He never once touched that look on her sand-mirror's face. As if that alone was already perfect.

She sat on the sand leaning back against her pack. Others had arrived without her really noticing. The beach was crowded. The event manager had put up a line of stakes with orange tape from one to the next to keep the growing crowds from coming too close. She was one of the only non-sculptors inside the barrier.

The Day of the Dead figure was done. Its colors garish, almost painful to the eye in the morning light. The sculptor smoothed here and there, but that was all.

The Egyptian obelisk had collapsed in the night. The

sculptor had stopped at the orange-tape border, stared at it for perhaps thirty seconds, then walked away without a word.

The castles were impressive in size, but they were simply castles. A gigantic school of leaping fish was wonderful in concept, but rough in execution. Still, very dramatic.

The best of the others was an arcing orca with a massive octopus in its jaws. The too-real, sand-brown tentacles stretched back along the orca, still fighting for purchase, struggling to do damage. It was dramatic and would be an easy winner.

If not for Morgan's sailboat. The level of precision and detail showed his mastery was beyond all of the others. Though that was only a piece of it.

No one could have missed that the boat of sand matched the one of fiberglass, aluminum, and Dacron moored offshore. Fewer, far fewer as she kept her sunhat pulled low, noted that she was the model for the skipper.

Instead, she could hear all of the whispered comments at the orange tape line close behind her that he'd captured the true spirit of Gloucester.

That unchanging face.

The statue had been a memorial back in 1923 on the three-hundredth anniversary of the founding of the city. *They that go down to the sea in ships.* In honor of the hundreds of fisherman who had lost their lives fishing from this port.

For a century since, that bronze skipper had stared out of the harbor, ready to fight the storm.

Battling, perhaps past reason, because that was

simply what one did. She knew that place. When the storm wracked the boat. Double-reef on the main. Nothing but a small Number Four jib for a headsail. No autopilot could manage such chaos. Adjustments were made to each wave approach with the lone goal of protecting the boat. Nothing to do but survive the storm.

Grim determination. That was expression of the Gloucester Fisherman's Memorial.

But Morgan had given her lips the slightest hint of a smile. Little more than a Mona Lisa smile, yet it changed everything. *Bring it on!*

Not sailing alone in fevered grim determination. But also in...hope? Perhaps too strong a word. Maybe...possibility?

A covert glance showed that more and more people had come to gather opposite his sculpture and watch his finishing touches. A clear crowd favorite. Yet he remained oblivious to the attention, staying focused on making the perfect even better until she couldn't stand it any longer.

"Stop! Just...stop!"

10

MORGAN FELT AS IF ALL THE STRINGS THAT HAD KEPT HIS arms in motion were cut at once.

His hands dropped to his side. The tools slipped from his nerveless fingers to tumble upon the sand with soft plops. He spit out the short length of surgical tube.

Then his legs let go and he collapsed onto the sand beside Mary.

But he didn't need to turn to see her expression, her thoughts. They were writ so clear upon the sand before him. He knew this person better than he knew himself.

Yes, the memory of her had held him upright through many, and even grim, challenges. Seeing her dream floating offshore, manifested into reality through pure willpower had told him the rest. She too had persevered through her own joys and failures. A quick search on his phone that first night had shown the mark she had slashed across the yachting world.

Women didn't do that. Not to the old boys' club. Except Mary Elizabeth didn't compete "like a girl," she competed like a skipper. Like someone who was in perfect command of who she was.

Making that jibe with the woman he'd risen from the sea, not so unlike Botticelli's Venus, had been the true challenge. Finding that vision, that emotion—the tough competitor, competing with no one harder than she did with herself, had been the true challenge.

Not proud. Not afraid.

He knew he'd really achieved a life's goal when his hands had carved the face he couldn't put words or emotion to. Compared to the rest of the sculpture, it was the least polished but he hadn't dared touch it for fear of ruining the whole. Sitting now, looking up at her in the sand, he could see it was that *im*perfection that made it so powerful. That made it seem to leap forward into the world past all of the real-world elements of boat, sail, and storm. That made it shine in the sand.

"I've never done anything like this before."

"It's...incredible, Morgan. Really incredible."

He had to blink several times before he could break the hypnosis and turn to look at her. "Did you just call me by my first name?"

She scoffed. "I've done that a bunch of times."

He shook his head slowly. "Not even the first day we met at the beginning of grade school. I'd remember. You're the one who tagged me as the Backward Pirate the first day, I hadn't even heard of Sir Henry Morgan yet and you had already tagged me with him."

Now she was the one blinking hard. "I did?"

"Day One," he assured her.

"And is this what backward pirates do, make sailboats

out of sand?" Her teases always made him want to laugh. Would this time too, if the question hadn't been at the heart of everything.

"Up until now." He began gathering the tools that had landed about his feet, brushing them clean, and slipping them into his toolbelt. When she still didn't speak, he concentrated on digging the sand out from under his fingernails. It didn't matter how short he kept them; sand always found a way to wedge in.

"*Need a hand?*" she said almost dreamily when she finally spoke.

He didn't look up.

"What happened, Morgan?" Mary Elizabeth Thomas had never been stupid.

He tried to shrug it off but she wouldn't let him. So as the final afternoon wound down—he told her.

How he'd survived school by immersing himself in the art crowd, eventually learning enough taekwondo to defend himself physically and ignoring the rest. The death of his parents. The fact that he was starting over.

"If I win this—"

Mary scoffed at his *if*.

"It pays off the last of the medical debts. Maybe enough for a fresh start, though I'll be damned if I know at what."

"This?" she nodded toward his sculpture as if it was a worthy goal in and of itself. Only Dad and fellow maniacs like Romero ever believed that.

"Maybe. I like doing it. But I haven't done anything else—ever. Hell, Mary, you've raced all over the world. Except for an intense block of days sand castling here and there, I haven't been past Marblehead in years. In my life, I guess. With Mom and Dad no longer anchoring me here, I'm starting to look up at the horizon. And when I do..." he looked up.

She waited him out.

He waved a hand at her sailboat. "When I do look up, I see that gorgeous boat sailed by my favorite woman in the world, ready to leap into the future. What do I do? *That!*" He waved his hand at his sculpture in disgust. "I can take reality and make it mundane."

"You can take a dream and show it to others." Then her voice dropped to a whisper he could barely hear. "You showed it to me."

He could feel the time was growing short. The judges were gathering at the far end of the works. Mary was sitting against a knapsack of fresh supplies. She'd be gone by sunrise. She'd be gone if he so much as blinked. Somehow, he'd held her here one last day with his portrait of her, but that wouldn't hold. It was all carved in sand.

"*Need a hand?* you asked. Do you sail, Backward Morgan?"

"Almost every day since you left. Had a Laser and won most races down in Marblehead with her. Yet another thing I had to sell when Dad got sick. I was a fair foredeck hand on a J/24—other people's. Never quite put together having one myself."

The judges were drawing closer. They sounded like a good group, not rushing through the afternoon. Instead they spent time with each artist, making kind noises. Offering tips and occasionally commiseration where called for. When an entire castle turret splattered them with its abrupt collapse, they'd laughed and assured the sculptor that they'd be judging it on the pre-collapse state even though it wasn't quite five o'clock yet.

The tone for the contest was fun and success.

But what was the tone here at the base of his female mariner?

Again Mary was all whispers, "I received a phone call last night—"

"Crap!" He scrambled to his knees and crawled over to the stern of the sand boat.

"I—" she sounded like she was strangling on something. The judges were approaching Romero's sculpture, the last one before his.

He took the time for a single calming breath. Then he began carving faster than he ever had in his life.

11
————

CAUGHT HALFWAY TO MAKING AN INSANE SUGGESTION, Mary didn't know whether to be thrilled or annoyed at being cut off.

Morgan was back in his intense mode. Tools in either hand, surgical tube in his mouth, spray bottle close to hand.

The judges had slowed at Romero's to discuss coloring techniques, earning their own on-the-spot master class much to the interest of the watching crowd that had been moving down the line with them.

Still Morgan worked. Not frantically, but without a wasted thought or motion. Without so much as a *sorry* or a *hold on* to her.

He was still carving when the judges finished with Romero and came up to him. He ignored them as thoroughly as he ignored her.

From their vantage, they saw something that amused them. Their eyes flickering from the boat, to her image, to what he was carving into the stern. Then one of them focused on her and quickly whispered to the others. All three looked at her closely then nodded with knowing smiles. Yep, she'd been pegged as Morgan's model.

And still Morgan the backward pirate carved.

When at last he finished, he flopped from his squat to sit. But the judges had moved too close and, in sitting, he knocked two of them to the sand. The third one waved a hand to her to come look.

As she rose, the rest of the crowd began to murmur and point. She was going to have to murder Morgan. That worked, she supposed as he was a backward pirate and it was only appropriate for the damsel to do *him* in.

She circled until she stood staring at the name he'd carved into the back of the sand boat. *The Mariner* in an arc of perfectly chiseled letters above a smaller port of call, *The World.* And in between them, he'd added her form, stretched out in full mermaid pose.

It wasn't the fish tail or the overlong hair masking the obviously naked breasts that stopped her. It was the smile. It was the view of the *possible* that lay upon the features of the image of herself in sand gripping the wheel—but made certain. Made real.

He still sat with his butt on the sand, looking at her, not at the judges or what he'd done. Asking a simple question that was everything, *Need a hand?*

She'd sailed alone metaphorically and actually for most of her life. Somehow, for reasons beyond her understanding, Morgan Henry understood that about her.

It would be simple to call Florida. They wanted her on the team badly enough, she could convince them to give Morgan the same thirty-day tryout. She knew what it meant to be a frequent winner at Marblehead; that had been a hard climb for her as well.

Yes, there was the solo Laser class of racing at the Olympics, she'd expected to excel in the women's division there. But there were also the 470s and the catamaran Nacra 17s requiring a mixed man-woman crew of two.

There were also deep-ocean races that called for a big boat like hers but allowed for a crew. Or perhaps she could give herself permission to simply stop now and then. Sail to Australia for a sand sculpting contest, it was less than two months away by boat, after all.

She didn't know what else Morgan Henry the Backward Pirate could see in her but he apparently liked whatever it was as his smile matched both hers and the hopeful mermaid carved in the sand.

———

If you enjoyed this story
please consider leaving a review.
They really help.

Keep reading for an exciting excerpt from:
Where Dreams #1: *Where Dreams are Born*

WHERE DREAMS ARE BORN (EXCERPT)

IF YOU ENJOYED THAT, YOU'LL LOVE
THIS TALE!

WHERE DREAMS ARE BORN
(EXCERPT)

RUSSELL LEANED HIS BACK AGAINST THE STUDIO DOOR after he locked it behind the last of the staff. He barely managed the energy to turn off his camera.

He knew it was good. The images were there; he'd really captured them.

But something was missing.

The groove ran so clean when he slid into it. First his Manhattan high-ceilinged loft would fade into the background, then the strobe lights, reflector umbrellas, and green-screen backdrops all became texture and tone.

Image, camera, and man then became one and nothing else mattered—a single flow of light, beginning before time was counted, and ending its journey in the printed image. One ray of primordial light traveling forever to glisten off the BMW roadster still parked in one corner of the rough-planked wood floor worn smooth by generations of use. Another ray lost in the dark blackness of the finest leather bucket seats. A hundred more picking out the supermodel's perfect hand dangling a single shining and golden key—the image shot just slow enough that the key blurred as it spun, but the logo remained clear.

He couldn't quite put his finger on it...

It would be another great ad by Russell Morgan, Inc. The client would be knocked dead—the ad leaving all others standing still as it roared down the passing lane. This one might get him another Clio, or even a second Mobius.

But...

There wasn't usually a "but."

And there definitely wasn't supposed to be one.

The groove had definitely been there, but he hadn't been in it.

That was the problem. It had slid along, sweeping his staff into their own orchestrated perfection, but he'd remained untouched. That ideal, seamless flow hadn't included him at all.

"Be honest, boyo, that session sucked," he told the empty studio. Everything had come together so perfectly for yet another ad for yet another high-end glossy. *Man, the Magazine* would launch spectacularly in a few weeks, a high-profile mid-December launch, and it would include a never before seen twelve-page spread by the great Russell Morgan. The rag would probably never pay off the lavish launch party of hope, ice sculptures, and chilled magnums of champagne before disappearing like a thousand before it.

"Morose much?"

The studio kept its thoughts to itself—the first reliable sign that he wasn't totally losing his shit.

He stowed the last camera with the others piled by his computer. At the breaker box he shut off the umbrellas, spots, scoops, and washes. The studio shifted from a stark landscape in hard-edged relief to a nest of curious shadows and rounded forms. The tang of hot metal and deodorant were the only lasting result of the day's efforts.

"Get your shit together, Russell." His reflection in the darkened window, stories above the streetlights of West 10th, was unimpressed and proved it was wise enough to not answer back. There was never a "down" after a shoot; there was always an "up."

Not tonight.

He'd kept everyone late—even though it was Thanksgiving eve—hoping for that smooth slide of image-camera-man. It was only when he saw the power of the images he captured that he knew he wasn't a part of the chain anymore and decided he'd paid enough triple-time expenses.

The next to last two-page spread would be the killer —shot with the door open against a background as black as the sports car's finish, the model's single perfect leg wrapped in thigh-high red-leather boots all that was visible in the driver's seat. The sensual juxtaposition of woman and sleek machine served as an irresistible focus. It was an ad designed to wrap every person with even a hint of a Y-chromosome around its little finger. And those with only X-chromosomes would simply want to be her. He'd shot a perfect combo of sex for the guys and power for the women.

Even the final one-page image, a close-up of driver's seat from exactly the same angle, revealing not the model but instead a single rose of precisely the same hue as the leather boot, hadn't moved him despite its perfection.

Without him noticing, Russell had become no more than the observer, merely a technician behind the camera. Now that he faced it, months, maybe even a year had passed since he'd been yanked all the way into the light-image-camera-man slipstream. Tonight was a wakeup call and he didn't like it one bit. Wakeup calls happened to others, not him. But tonight he could no longer ignore it, he hadn't even trailed along in the churned-up wake.

"You're just a creative cog in the advertising machine." Ouch! That one stung, but it didn't turn aside the relentless steamroller of his thoughts speeding down some empty, godforsaken autobahn.

His career was roaring ahead, his business' growth running fast and smooth. But, now that he considered it, he really didn't give a damn.

His life looked perfect, but—"Don't think it!"—his autobahn mind finished despite the command, *it wasn't.*

Russell left his silent reflection to its own thoughts and went through the back door that led to his apartment —closing it tightly on the perfect BMW, the perfect rose, and somewhere, lost among a hundred other props from dozens of other shoots, the long pair of perfect red-leather Chanel boots that had been wrapped around the most expensive legs in Manhattan. He didn't care if he never walked back through that door again. He'd been doing his art by rote; how god-awful sad was that?

And just to rub salt in the wound, he shot *commercial* art.

He'd never had the patience to do art for art's sake. Delayed gratification was his idea of no fun at all. He left the apartment dark with only the city's soft glow through the blind-covered windows revealing the vaguest outlines of the framed art on the wall. Even that almost overwhelmed him tonight.

He didn't want to see the huge prints by the *art* artists: autographed Goldsworthy, Liebowitz, and Joseph Francis' photomosaics for the moderns. A hundred and fifty rare, even one-of-a-kind prints adorned his walls—all the way back through Bourke-White to Russell's prize, an original Daguerre. The Museum of Modern Art kept begging to borrow his collection for a show...and at the moment he was half tempted to dump the whole lot in their Dumpster if they didn't want it.

Crossing the one-room loft apartment—as spacious as the studio—he bypassed the circle of avant-garde chairs that were almost as uncomfortable as they looked and avoided the lush black-leather wrap-around sectional sofa of such ludicrous scale that it could be a playpen for two or host a party for twenty. He cracked the fridge in the stainless-steel-and-black corner kitchen searching for something other than his usual beer.

A bottle of Krug.

Maybe he was just being grouchy after a long day's work.

Juice.

No. He'd run his enthusiasm into the ground but good.

Milk even.

Would he miss the camera if he never picked it up again?

No reaction.

Nothing.

Not even an itch in his palm.

That was an emptiness he did not want to face. Especially not alone, in his apartment, in the middle of the world's most vibrant city.

Russell turned away, and just as the door swung closed, the last sliver of light—the relentless chilly blue-white of the refrigerator bulb—shone across his bed. A quick grab snagged the edge of the door and left the narrow beam illuminating a long pale form on his black-silk bedspread.

The Chanel boots weren't in the studio after all. They were still wrapped around those three thousand dollar-an-hour legs: the only clothing on a perfect body. Five foot-eleven of intensely toned female anatomy right down to an exquisitely stair-mastered behind. Her long, white-blonde hair lay as a perfect Godiva over her tanned breasts—except for their too exact symmetry, even the closest inspection didn't reveal the work done there. She lay with one leg raised just ever so slightly to hide what was meant to be revealed later.

Melanie.

By the steady rise and fall of her flat stomach, he knew she'd fallen asleep while waiting for him to finish in the studio.

How long had they been an item? Two months? Three?

She'd made him feel alive...at least when he was

actually with her. Melanie was the super-model in his bed or on his arm at yet another SoHo gallery opening. Together they journeyed to sharp parties and trendy three-star restaurants where she dazzled and wooed yet another gathering of New York's finest with her ever so soft, so sensual, and so studied French accent. Together they were wired into the heart of the in-crowd.

But that wasn't him, was it? It didn't sound like the Russell he once knew.

Perhaps "they" were about how *he* looked on *her* arm?

Did she know tomorrow was the annual Thanksgiving ordeal at his parents? The grand holiday gathering that he'd rather die than attend? Any number of eligible woman would be floating about his parents' house out in Greenwich; anyone able to finagle an invitation would attend in hopes of snaring one of *People Magazine's* "100 Most Eligible." They all wanted to land the heir to a billion or some such; though he was wealthy enough on his own, by his own sweat, to draw anyone's attention. He ranked number twenty-four on the list this year—up from forty-seven the year before despite Tom Cruise being available yet again.

But not Melanie. He knew that it wasn't the money that drew her. Yes, she wanted him. But even more, she wanted the life that came with him—wrapped in the man-package. She wanted The Life. The one that *People Magazine* readers dreamed about between glossy pages.

His fingertips were growing cold where they held the refrigerator door cracked open.

If he woke her there'd be amazing sex. Or a great party to go to. Or...

Did he want "Or"? What more did he want from her?

Sex. Companionship. An energy, a vivacity, a thirst he feared that he lacked. Yes.

But where was that smooth synchronicity hiding, like the light-image-camera-man of photography that he'd lost? Where lurked that perfect flow from one person to another? Did she feel it? Could he ever feel it? Did it even exist?

"More?" he whispered into the darkness to test the sound. He knew all about wanting more.

The refrigerator door slid shut—escaping from his numbed fingers—which plunged the apartment back into darkness, taking Melanie along with it.

His breath echoed in the vast darkness. Proof that he was alive if nothing more.

It was time to close the studio—time to be done with Russell Incorporated.

Then what?

Maybe Angelo would know what to do. He always claimed that he did. Maybe this time Russell would actually listen to his almost-brother, though he knew from the experience of being himself for the last thirty years that was unlikely.

Seattle.

Damn! He'd have to go to bloody Seattle to find his best friend. There was a possible upside to such a trip—maybe there'd be a flight out before tomorrow's mess at his parents'. He slapped his pocket, but once again he'd set his phone down in some unknown corner of the studio and it would take forever to find. He really needed two—one chained down so that he could always find it to call the other.

Russell considered the darkness. He could guarantee that Seattle wouldn't be a big hit with Melanie.

Now if he only knew whether that was a good thing or bad.

———

Keep reading now!
A great tale of romance and adventure,
Of sailboats, food, fashion, and fun.
Available at fine retailers everywhere.
Where Dreams are Born

And please don't forget that review for Solo Passage.

ABOUT THE AUTHOR

USA Today and Amazon #1 Bestseller M. L. "Matt" Buchman has 70+ action-adventure thriller and military romance novels, 100 short stories, and lotsa audiobooks. PW says: "Tom Clancy fans open to a strong female lead will clamor for more." Booklist declared: "3X Top 10 of the Year." A project manager with a geophysics degree, he's designed and built houses, flown and jumped out of planes, solo-sailed a 50' sailboat, and bicycled solo around the world...and he quilts. More at: www.mlbuchman.com.

Other works by M. L. Buchman: *(* - also in audio)*

Action-Adventure Thrillers

Dead Chef
One Chef!
Two Chef!

Miranda Chase
*Drone**
*Thunderbolt**
*Condor**
*Ghostrider**
*Raider**
*Chinook**
*Havoc**
*White Top**
*Start the Chase**
*Lightning**

Science Fiction / Fantasy

Deities Anonymous
Cookbook from Hell: Reheated
Saviors 101

Single Titles
Monk's Maze
the Me and Elsie Chronicles

Contemporary Romance

Eagle Cove
Return to Eagle Cove
Recipe for Eagle Cove
Longing for Eagle Cove
Keepsake for Eagle Cove

Love Abroad
Heart of the Cotswolds: England
Path of Love: Cinque Terre, Italy

Where Dreams
Where Dreams are Born
Where Dreams Reside
*Where Dreams Are of Christmas**
Where Dreams Unfold
Where Dreams Are Written
Where Dreams Continue

Non-Fiction

Strategies for Success
Managing Your Inner Artist/Writer
*Estate Planning for Authors**
Character Voice
Narrate and Record Your Own
*Audiobook**

Short Story Series by M. L. Buchman:

Action-Adventure Thrillers

Dead Chef

Miranda Chase Origin Stories

Romantic Suspense

Antarctic Ice Fliers

US Coast Guard

Contemporary Romance

Eagle Cove

Other

Deities Anonymous (fantasy)

Single Titles

The Emily Beale Universe
(military romantic suspense)

The Night Stalkers
MAIN FLIGHT
The Night Is Mine
I Own the Dawn
Wait Until Dark
Take Over at Midnight
Light Up the Night
Bring On the Dusk
By Break of Day
Target of the Heart
Target Lock on Love
Target of Mine
Target of One's Own
NIGHT STALKERS HOLIDAYS
*Daniel's Christmas**
*Frank's Independence Day**
*Peter's Christmas**
Christmas at Steel Beach
*Zachary's Christmas**
*Roy's Independence Day**
*Damien's Christmas**
Christmas at Peleliu Cove

Henderson's Ranch
*Nathan's Big Sky**
*Big Sky, Loyal Heart**
*Big Sky Dog Whisperer**
*Tales of Henderson's Ranch**

Shadow Force: Psi
*At the Slightest Sound**
*At the Quietest Word**
*At the Merest Glance**
*At the Clearest Sensation**

White House Protection Force
*Off the Leash**
*On Your Mark**
*In the Weeds**

Firehawks
Pure Heat
Full Blaze
*Hot Point**
*Flash of Fire**
Wild Fire
SMOKEJUMPERS
*Wildfire at Dawn**
*Wildfire at Larch Creek**
*Wildfire on the Skagit**

Delta Force
*Target Engaged**
*Heart Strike**
*Wild Justice**
*Midnight Trust**

Emily Beale Universe Short Story Series
The Night Stalkers
The Night Stalkers Stories
The Night Stalkers CSAR
The Night Stalkers Wedding Stories
The Future Night Stalkers

Delta Force
Th Delta Force Shooters
The Delta Force Warriors

Firehawks
The Firehawks Lookouts
The Firehawks Hotshots
The Firebirds

White House Protection Force
Stories

Future Night Stalkers
Stories (Science Fiction)